the celtic circle

evelyn arslan

Published by **eNovella**, Perth, Western Australia

Cover Design by Tom Fisher

Typeset in Times New Roman.

National Library of Australia Cataloguing-in-Publication entry:

Author: Arslan, Evelyn.

Title: The Celtic circle [book] / Evelyn Arslan.

Edition: 2nd ed.

ISBN-10: 0-9872987-4-7, ISBN-13: 978-0-9872987-4-4 (soft cover)

Target Audience: For young adults

Dewey Number: A823.4

CHAPTERS

Come with me to the island of my childhood; a place of both beauty and of peril.

Imagine if you will, carefree summers spent amongst rock-pools; a world of crabs and starfish and pink and red sea-anemones. Rocks green and slippery with seaweed and the sea no further than a short walk away. Deep pools left by the outgoing tide; safe enough for us to bathe and splash till dusk. Soft-sanded dunes to climb and slide down, with our young eyes fixed on the far-off horizon.

If summer was tranquil, then winter was fierce! Winds howled as storms broke over sea at night. Safe in warm beds we lay, ever-fearful for those small fishing boats somewhere out there in that wild darkness. We knew the lurking dangers of this rocky shoreline.

Not far away lay the Holy Island of Lindisfarne: a place of drama; of religion and of violence. Secluded in solitude, monks once created illuminated manuscripts of the Gospels. Saint Cuthbert set forth from here to persuade northern tribes to abandon their Celtic gods and festivals. An island reached by causeway, but only when tidal waters would allow. Scary but exciting to the young were the swirling waters that rapidly engulfed and cut-off retreat from this strange island. The sorry tales of travellers lost before reaching safety must then be true!

But this island of contemplation and sanctuary was violently shaken when the first Viking raid violated this very shore. The priory was ransacked, the monks were slain; and a terror began that was to pervade the whole of the British Isles.

Eyes long ago had scanned these same horizons in great fear.

PART ONE

Chapter 1

It was the darkest of nights.

Iyannah lay on the floor close to her grandmother; but she didn't sleep. She could hear the wind from the sea make its circling gusts around their stone house. And she could hear the gaspings for breath that came sporadically from her grandmother.

From time to time, her grandmother stirred, and began to mumble the well-recited stories of their Celtic people, but in a low voice that was almost like a prayer:

"In those days our houses were made from young saplings and branches interwoven round and round. We left them behind and fled in times of danger. Danger came often but the gods always protected us."

Fearing that the fever had returned and that Grandma would continue incessantly with the much repeated stories of the history of their tribe, she dipped the soft cloth into the water jug and squeezed it with her hands before laying it gently on her grandmother's forehead.

"Hush, Grandma, you're safe here. Try and rest."

The coolness of the damp cloth seemed to help. Her grandmother gave her a fond smile.

"You're a good girl, Iyannah. We've always been close, you and I."

Relieved at these more lucid words, Iyannah was quick to respond.

"You were always there for me, Grandma. Remember when we went to gather berries in the woods that day, and we found those tiny red ones hidden in the grass near the brook. They tasted so sweet. That was such a perfect day."

"I remember too", smiled her grandmother.

"When you're well, we'll go back there, Grandma, you'll see."

"I don't think so", said Grandma calmly. "I'm an old woman. The gods should have taken me, and not young Aila."

Her grandmother had survived that harsh winter that had seen poor Aila die. And this last winter had not been as severe. Meagre rations were nothing new to her grandmother; she had eaten and drank little but she would sit close to the hearth.

She'd slept more often and when awake her thoughts had been far-off and not with her family.

"Don't talk like that, Grandma. Let me fetch you some herbal tea. I collected fresh herbs last evening. You'll be fine."

Iyannah loved her grandmother so much and it distressed her to see the changes that now overcame her. The fragile, shrivelled figure lying nearby no longer resembled the person she had always known. Only the eyes still held some brightness and her grandmother's mouth sometimes betrayed a fleeting smile as though in possession of a great secret that was pleasing to her. But Grandma was shaking her head.

"I don't fear Death, Iyannah. I have seen it too many times. But there is much I need to tell you …."

Her eyes now closed with the effort of speech and she sighed deeply.

3

Iyannah quickly held out the cup of the herbal brew so her grandmother could take a sip from it.

But Grandmother was now impatient and even agitated. She suddenly pushed the cup aside with the little strength that remained in her now thin and bony fingers. Iyannah was startled by this sudden movement and let the cup fall, spilling the liquid out onto the rush matting. She stepped back in alarm as her grandmother tried to raise herself up and now began to rock from side to side in rhythm to her recitation. Her voice rose as she continued her wonderful and frightening tales of heroes; of giants; and of terrifying monsters. Her eyes were open and she stared fixedly above Iyannah's head, up towards the round roof above. It was as if she had to finish this saga. She could not be calmed.

Iyannah was distressed. She felt powerless to stop this torrent of words. Her mother, heavily pregnant with her third child, came quickly and pulled back the dividing drapes of the sleeping area. She, too, was disconcerted by this change in the aged woman's behaviour. She sat beside Iyannah and reached out her hand to offer some comfort to the frightening figure moving and muttering there.

Once more, a calming gesture was forcibly rejected, and the hollow voice continued to intone the story:

"Behind every rock, every bush and every tree, we met warriors and monsters and demons; our enemies were both mortal and immortal. The gods gave us their signs and warnings. Without the gods we would not have survived."

Iyannah looked at her mother as they both realised that the frail figure was using her last throes of strength to recount the code of the ancestors, the elements she saw as vital for the survival of her people and that must be passed down. Anxious for young

4

Iyannah, her mother gave her a task that would take her away from this scene of so much anguish:

"Can you go and re-kindle the fire. Father will need to go to the pastures soon and the air is chill. I will sit with her now."

Iyannah was relieved to withdraw from this disturbing and never-ending incantation. In her mind she wanted to put her hands over her ears to block out the sounds and scream: Stop, Grandma, please stop!

She set some logs of wood from the central hearth onto the dying embers and stoked them back to life. She sat down on the small stool that was her grandmother's when she used to regale all and sundry with her fantastic tales. Her audience had become younger as the years passed: Iyannah, and her younger sister, who had died in that dreadful winter two years ago; Dani, with his curly black hair and smiling face and his two brothers, older and more solemn, but with the same dark good looks; and other children too, that would gather and sit in a semi-circle around her grandmother. As young children they had often become too frightened to move away and yet too afraid to listen.

But not as afraid as Iyannah felt that night. She could still hear her grandmother's voice. On and on it went:

"Once Great-grandfather outwitted a Roman escort bringing fresh supplies to the fort on the Wall. Hidden in the long grass with his companions, he saw the bright helmets of the soldiers and the wagon of food supplies. Together they watched and took their opportunity well and bravely. At night they descended silently and swiftly. Their escape was miraculous. They knew the terrain so well that pursuit by the Roman soldiers would have been foolish!"

Iyannah knew what followed. There was great feasting for the tribe after this. Straw helmets were made and the warriors danced and mocked the Romans that they had tricked. An even greater celebration had followed when the Romans suddenly left. Grandmother's eyes would shine reflecting the flickering light from the fire in the hearth as she relived the exploits of her people in a voice that half-sang; half-spoke the well-remembered words of family sagas:

"Great grandfather himself made sure that the Romans never came further into northern territory."

With a sudden jolt, she realised that her grandmother's voice had fallen silent. The sounds she heard were in her mind; in her memory. She made herself return to that bedside. Grandmother was now exhausted and her breathing was becoming increasingly laboured. She now looked directly at Iyannah and her eyes signalled for Iyannah to come closer. She was indicating a small wooden box that she always kept close to her. Iyannah picked it up and offered it to her grandmother.

"No", whispered her grandmother hoarsely, shaking her head. "You must keep it". Iyannah looked inside and saw the small blue-green stone: her Grandma's 'talisman' that had come long ago from a secret place. Her grandmother's fingers covered Iyannah's hand as she held the stone and a strange warmth emanated through her whole being. Did it come from the stone or from her grandmother's touch? Whichever it was, Iyannah recognised that a precious gift had been passed on to her and she felt the deep emotion of that moment.

Grandma relaxed her grip on Iyannah's hand and her breathing now became easier. "I am ready to go, now" she breathed softly and that secretive smile returned.

Her eyes would soon be closed forever and Iyannah knew her own childhood would be over; her life would never be the same.

Her mother went to bring in her father and Iyannah sat in the still dark room and gazed down on her grandmother's face. She seemed so peaceful and surprisingly, Iyannah almost felt a sense of elation that the worst would soon be over. She carefully put the talisman stone back into its wooden box.

As her father entered and made his way to his mother's bedside, Iyannah and her mother held tightly onto each other. Her father stood quietly for what seemed like hours but was really only several minutes. Then he nodded to his wife and gently kissed his mother's hand. Iyannah knew it was over. She left the house and, taking a loose cape with her, ran outside into the early morning mist.

Chapter 2

Dani, the master boat-builder's son, stood at the water's edge. His boat was prepared and he was ready to sail. The sea-fret would lift soon and thin slivers of light were slowly pointing upwards from the horizon. He was at the northern curve of the bay where the rocks were sharp and narrow and stretched out like a hag's long finger and crooked nail ever-pointing to the sea. Danger lay in the jagged rocks below the surface: far more treacherous than those in view. Beyond those rocks lay the wild moors of the north.

Dani loved the sea. All his family were sea-farers and expert boat-builders. His boat was flat-bottomed but with a high bow. The flatness of it meant it could easily be launched from the beach; whilst the high bow offered the resistance needed for any high waves which might otherwise sweep it away. He did not see himself as a 'fisherman' but as an adventurer and explorer: bringing back good supplies of fish was only incidental to young Dani's sea-journeys. He'd heard many tales of great monsters of the deep and he was sure that one day he too would find such a creature; overcome it; and return home like a hero from days gone by.

He checked again the small lines of twine and rolls of net. His paddle and his spear rested alongside and he was about to push his boat out from the beach when a movement behind him, to his right, caused him to stop. There was someone sliding and stumbling down the sand-dunes; someone who seemed to be in great distress.

Iyannah sat down; she could go no further. She was in a daze and had no idea how she had reached the beach. Yes, tears had threatened but they had not come. Grief seemed instead to have numbed all feeling. She shivered and pulled her cape more closely around her.

Her long brown hair was loose and unbraided. Wisps of curl formed on her forehead, twisted into tendrils by the dampness of the mist. She was bare-foot and was now realising that the sharp grasses of the dunes had cut and scratched at her feet and legs as she had scrambled downwards. Her right hand was burning, though, and as she opened it she could see a dull red mark in her palm: the imprint of Grandma's talisman stone.

She gazed at her hand in wonder and relived the moment that her Grandma had given that special stone to her. What did it mean? She'd always known that her grandmother had strange gifts; that she could 'read' signs and give warnings from the gods. Had her grandmother's insights come from that stone? Why had she insisted it must be given to her young grand-daughter?

She sensed that someone was moving towards her and turned in fright to see Dani standing quietly watching her. He did not speak; he seemed unsure whether or not to approach her. She put her head down and blinked hard to stop the tears that now indeed were falling. He listened to her quiet sobbing and at last he spoke.

"Is it your grandmother, Iyannah?"

She nodded and looked up at him through long eyelashes that were dark and wet with tears.

He looked at her with great concern in his eyes and leaned forward and put his hand gently on her shoulder.

"Don't cry, Iyannah. She would not want you to be so distressed."

Iyannah tried to speak, but sobs still choked her. She nodded, knowing that he was right. Her grandmother would want her to be brave; she would not want her to be upset. But Iyannah was torn apart by sorrow; by anger; by self-pity and even despair and it was hard to cope with these conflicting emotions.

She struggled to find her voice and give vent to her feelings.

"But, Dani, she was always there. When I was young she took care of me. She took me to fetch water from the stream. She showed me the sacred spring and taught me the prayer to the god of the Hills. She sang to me and told me stories; she comforted me and made me smile. I just can't imagine my life without her …"

Her voice gave up again, but she did not cry; she stared bleakly at the sea. Dani was silent for a moment and seemed to be choosing his words carefully.

"I know how you must feel, Iyannah, but your grandmother was greatly respected, greatly loved. She will be missed by so many of our people. They will come to visit at this sad time. Your mother and father will need you to be there. They will need your help and they will need you to be strong."

Iyannah knew this to be true. There would be little time for private grief. People would come and Iyannah would need to be there to help receive them and see that her mother found time to rest as the new baby would soon be due.

Iyannah sat upright and sighed deeply. She was reluctant to move. "You have to go, Iyannah"

Dani spoke again and put his hand to her to her cheek as though wiping a stray tear. Iyannah stood up and looked directly at him. She had known Dani all her life; they had been young children together. But that seemed so long ago.

"Go back and see what needs to be done," he continued. "I'll be back here at sunset and I'll wait and meet you, if you like. If you need my help, I will be here for you."

Suddenly, Iyannah gave him a sweet but fleeting smile.

She turned and saying, "I must go", she reached out and grasped Dani's hand, but for only a second.

She knew he was watching as she made her way up from the beach. She saw as he half-turned to walk back to his boat.

She reached the top of the sand dune by the time he was pushing his boat out into the water. She stopped to look back at him. At the same moment, they both raised their hands and waved. She watched the small boat bob out on the waves and remembered his words: you have to go back, Iyannah.

One last look and then she turned, took a deep breath and made her way home.

Chapter 3

Iyannah's father, Jalb, was waiting outside their home as she made her way back from the high sand dunes. Their home, a small stone building like the others around it, was set well back from the coast-line. Here the land was level. Pasture land and small plots for the growing of cereals and vegetables were neatly set out behind the close- knit collection of houses. The land beyond gently rose upwards and became more wooded but a well-worn path between the trees and bushes led to the fresh-water spring and a small brook that caught the plentiful water that cascaded from the hills beyond. The hills themselves were dark and craggy and were cloud-topped in all seasons. This place had been given the name 'Craghburn' when the settlement had first been made there.

Jalb spoke softly; he too was in grief.

"I've told your mother to rest. I need to see to the cattle, but I won't stay long. Your Aunt Mila is here. She will need your help, Iyannah."

Her father had never been her grandmother's favourite. He was not of the 'heroic' mould. His two elder brothers had quickly become bored with the more settled life of the little community and had left years ago to fight for various Northumbrian kings. The sudden departure of the Romans had left a vacuum and many a Northumbrian king had found to his cost how difficult that was to fill. Wars seemed to be forever ongoing and her grandmother loved to listen to news of her 'warrior sons' and hear of their exploits even if they had now become in reality mere 'mercenaries', involved in many devious plots as new kings of Northumbria were regularly overthrown and 'would-be pretenders' took over. Iyannah was not so impressed: they rarely visited and her father was a good man and worked hard for his family.

Over long years, she had watched his strong hands and stubby fingers handle tiny seedlings with such care and gentleness. Jalb knew the best times to sow; the best time of day to water; how and when to protect young plants from frosts that came even in Spring. He knew when to harvest to ensure the best yield possible for his family and those with them in their community.

A short, stocky man, who talked little but thought deeply, Jalb had been sorely distressed by the death of her younger sister. It had been a harsh winter that year, and food shortages meant that many had died. Aila had had too little strength in her thin body to fight off the fever when it came. Now Jalb spent long hours nurturing the grain and vegetable crops hoping that sufficient food could be stored for the hard times that each winter brought. He never wanted any of his family to suffer such a fate again.

Iyannah smiled as she remembered how her father would tease her grandmother about her "superstitious nonsense." He had loved to provoke her. But Iyannah knew that her father always made sure that the first milk taken each day from their small herd of cows was carefully placed in a dish at the special place for the Little People, to appease them. And she herself had helped him place rowan branches in the pen of sickly calves to aid their recovery and ensure healthy cattle. Jalb did not take any chances.

Aunt Mila was round and plump, of the same stocky build as her brother. She was a kindly soul and came quickly to embrace Iyannah.

"Don't worry, Iyannah. I am sure you and I can cope. Your mother is sleeping. I've put the griddle pan to heat so we'll have oatcakes for any visitors. The Lamenters will come tomorrow, but only close friends will come today."

She stood back and looked at Iyannah.

"Where on earth have you been? Your legs are all scratched; your hair needs braiding; and you need a clean set of clothes! I know you're upset but we have to make ready. Take some water and I'll manage till you change."

"Don't worry about your grandmother. I've seen to her," she added, seeing Iyannah's anxious glance to the place where her grandmother lay.

Iyannah was glad that Aunt Mila was there. As she washed her face she thought: Dani must have thought I looked dreadful. Maybe I will go and see him later, and she felt reassured by the thought.

Chapter 4

Iyannah was surprised to hear sounds of laughter coming from outside the house. She went out and found her mother had joined Aunt Mila, and also two elderly women, who she vaguely recognised as old friends of her grandmother. They were sitting around the outdoor oven on which the griddle was placed.

Seeing Iyannah's puzzled expression, the oldest lady there began to explain. "Don't worry, Iyannah. We're only talking about your grandmother when she was young. She was an amazing child, you know."

"I'm learning things I didn't know," said Iyannah's mother. "Come and sit with us, here."

Iyannah knelt on the ground by her mother's side.

"Well," said the oldest lady, continuing her story," she was only about seven years old when she kept having the same dream. She had it for three nights, one after the other. At last her father decided to take her to the chief to see what he thought. Your grandmother had no fear in talking to the chief. She told him of her dream."

"What was her dream?" asked Iyannah.

"I was coming to that," continued the old lady.

She now began to mimic Iyannah's grandmother in a child's voice.

"'Sir, I dreamt of a strange bird. It spread out its wings and flew down and laid an egg beside an old well. The egg then seemed to turn to stone. Other leaves and feathers near the well had also turned to stone, but they were an ashen white. The bird's egg stayed blue and green and speckled but it was now turned to stone. A strange hand, larger than a man's hand, then began to dig with its sharp nails beneath the egg. Then in the hole made by the hand, there appeared a round black metal pot. And inside it were many golden coins.'

"Whatever did the chief think of her?" Iyannah wanted to know.

"Well, the chief listened carefully and observed her closely. He could hear that she was earnest in her speech and something about her led him to trust her. It seemed to

be no childish fantasy. At last, he spoke, 'I do know of such a well. I will send my men to search. I think your dream is sent by the gods. You must wait here till they return.' And you'll never believe it! It all came true! They found a blue-green shiny stone just like an egg by the old well and also a pot of gold coins, just as your grandmother had said."

Iyannah was truly shocked by this. A blue-green stone? The one she had been given? Aunt Mila ended the story:

"And the chief was so pleased that he gave the stone to your grandmother and he also betrothed her to his grandson that very day. Your grandmother lived in the chief's house from that day on and he always spoke with her before he made any plans." "And it was your grandfather who brought us all to this place, to Craghburn," added her mother.

Craghburn was their haven of refuge: food supplemented with the fruits that the ocean could provide; fresh water; good soil for cultivation; stone to build more permanent houses; and trees to cut down for the fires needed in the cold months. "But," said the other old friend," it was your grandmother that decided that this was the place for us. Where the god of the Hills touches the sky and where the Sea-god touches the land are sacred places and Craghburn is between them both."

Iyannah thought for a moment. It sounded so strange.

"But where did the gold come from," she asked, "and what happened to it?"

For Iyannah knew her people were poor.

Aunt Mila explained, "We think that pirates had put the gold there and marked the place with the strange stone. Our chief used the gold to bribe warring tribes who were reluctant to allow us to cross their land. We were able to come here without too much blood-shed."

"I didn't know any of this," said Iyannah's mother," but I do know that the stone was special. Grandma used to gather herbs for potions and healing remedies. She used to hold the stone as she listened to people who came to her for help. And then she could choose the right herbs for each person's need. She always kept the stone near to her." "But, Mama, why did she give the stone to me?"

"I don't know the answer to that," her mother replied. "Perhaps when you are older you will find a way to use it, too."

And so the afternoon passed in conversation that left Iyannah in little doubt that her grandmother had indeed been a very special person.

As the sun began to move lower in the sky, Iyannah told her mother that she would fetch fresh water from the brook and quickly left the old ladies to their memories.

Chapter 5

Iyannah, however, did not go immediately to the brook. Instead she made her way to the top of the sand dunes and looked down to see if Dani's boat had returned. But before she could pick out his boat, she saw Dani standing at the shore-line looking upwards. Even at that distance, Iyannah could see that he was anxiously looking for her. He smiled and waved, and as she did not come down to the beach, he began to climb the steep path up to the top.

Suddenly Iyannah felt nervous. She felt amazed at her own daring in contriving this ruse to see him. (Well, I owe him for his kindness this morning, she told herself.) Dani was breathless as he reached the top and came to her side. To cover her embarrassment, Iyannah now began to talk rapidly and gave Dani little chance to speak.

"I can't stay long," she began, "I have to go to the brook. I just wanted to tell you that

I am coping and to say thank you for this morning." She talked without really looking at him.

But Dani was not having that.

"I will walk with you, then. And then we can talk for longer."

Iyannah was astonished at this. Fetching water from the brook was 'women's work' and men rarely walked up there.

Still, it was a pleasing offer, so together they made their way past the houses and out towards the pastures.

"I didn't know my grandmother had so many special gifts," began Iyannah. "She was only young when she was betrothed to the grandson of a chief. And it was my grandfather who first came to this place."

Dani knew that her grandfather had been a great warrior; in fact, unlike Iyannah he could remember when her grandfather died.

"Please tell me about it, Dani. I want to know everything."

"I was about six years old when your grandfather died," began Dani. "I knew that something special was taking place. Torches were lit and placed outside all the houses. For seven days there was wailing from the womenfolk, and on the last day old warriors came here to tell of the greatness of their fallen comrade. They told the story of the great victories they had won over their enemies in the past. Then they carried his body in procession to the high place where it could be burned. All the people carried torches and followed, throwing them onto the bonfire in respect and to scare off any evil, dark powers so the great warrior could make his passage to the Otherworld. It is said that great warriors are re-born and return to help their tribe in times of trouble."

"Do you believe that, Dani?"

"I don't know but it is possible. I would like to think so."

They climbed the steep hill up through the woodlands and reached the brook quickly. Then Iyannah went ahead, as always, to pay homage to the Sacred Spring and offer a prayer of thanksgiving to the god of the Hills. A rowan tree grew beside this spring; a tree revered for it offered protection from evil spirits. Brightly coloured pieces of woven cloth were tied to some of its branches, votive gifts from those desiring curses to be lifted and health restored. Iyannah stretched out her cupped hands and took enough of the sacred water to bathe her face and neck. It felt cool and refreshing.

Then she went back to the brook and filled the water-carrier before turning to go back down the woodland path.

She knew Dani was watching her closely and indeed he was smiling at her graceful movements. Her hands were so tiny beside his, yet they moved deftly and quickly to fill the water-jug, a task that she had carried out daily from being very young. She refused his offer to carry the jug, but accepted his suggestion that they sit for a while and watch the sun going down behind the dark hills.

As ever, there were clouds over the hills, clouds which intruded over the sun's face from time to time as they watched.

"My grandmother could read 'signs' in strange cloud shapes, you know," asserted

Iyannah, "and in shadows that crossed the sun."

"She was a clever woman, there's no doubt," agreed Dani.

"And she listened to the sharp cry of any bird nearby, lest that was a message from the gods."

"I love watching the sea-birds, out there," said Dani, pointing towards the distant shore-line. "I learn where the fish are hiding if I watch the birds diving and catching their prey. I have seen birds with beaks like rainbows. You would love to see them." "No, I wouldn't," Iyannah shuddered," I don't like the sea. I much prefer it here on the hillside."

Dani laughed, "But I love the sea. It changes so quickly, not like your hills. It makes for great adventure. Like the heroes of old used to have."

Iyannah was not convinced, but did not say so, for she had seen her father making his way back from the pastures. And she realised that it was now almost dark.

"Oh, Dani, we must go. My father is heading home. I have to take the water."

Dani reached out his hand to help her up and so it was that they returned, still hand in hand, down the hill and back to the houses.

"I won't be able to see you, tomorrow," said Dani. "My father has two more boats to repair and I promised to help him."

"I think I'll be very busy, too", said Iyannah wryly.

"I know," added Dani, "but if you always fetch water at this same time in the evening, I will come when I can."

"I will do that, then," smiled Iyannah, "I think I can manage it." "And I will do my best, too," smiled Dani.

They parted as the houses separated out and Dani made to follow the seashore path down to the boatyard. Iyannah's house lay higher up. But again they both stopped, looked back and waved at the very same time.

Chapter 6

Iyannah awoke with her grandmother's wooden box and talisman still beside her. But the only dreams she had had were of Dani's face: his dark eyes looking at her with such caring and compassion. In the distance, she heard the low sound of a drumbeat, a sound that was coming nearer.

The Lamenters: she remembered, and got up quickly to dress and braid her hair. Aunt Mila and her mother were already busy preparing flat loaves of bread, and a pot of water was heating on the fire for the vegetable soup that would be needed to feed the elders of the tribe.

Iyannah was once more engulfed by sadness. Her grandmother was really gone, then. The ritual that would now follow held fears for her. Yesterday had been a day of happy memories; today would be a time of grief.

Her father came back with the spring vegetables he had freshly gathered, and Iyannah took them outside to wash and prepare. The slow drumbeat grew louder, and sounds of wailing and crying now accompanied it. The chopped vegetables were added to the pot and her mother put in the herbs that would flavour the soup.

Then she and Aunt Mila, Iyannah and her father stood outside their house and awaited the arrival of the 'official' mourners. Iyannah shivered, but it was from apprehension rather than the chill of the morning breeze.

People from nearby houses, too, stood outside and waited, showing their respect. The noise grew louder, the drumbeat more insistent; the exaggerated weeping and wailing was reaching a crescendo. The drumming stopped and the Lamenters were there, at the threshold of their small house.

The men, (the oldest in their community), came to her father to offer remorse and condolence. The women gathered around Aunt Mila and Iyannah's mother. It seemed that Iyannah was invisible. Her day passed in a whirl of fetching drinks; baking yet more bread; and stirring and serving more and more soup. She heard an old man telling her father that messages had been sent out to others who knew her grandmother, but who had split away forming new settlements in other areas. More people will be coming: she thought.

Suddenly, there was silence, and then, with the lone drum setting the rhythm, the

Story-teller spokesman began his narrative.

"In a time before time, the gods moved over the waters ...."

His story was a historic record of their people: of their voyages over strange seas, and long journeys over many lands. It was a tale of hardship, but also one of humour and survival. Great heroes were named and their amazing feats and victories recalled.

'Betrayers', or those who offended the gods, or the chiefs, were accused once more. Their 'crimes' were never to be forgotten. The delivery was perfect; the themes consistent: never forget the gods who guided and protected us.

And then he spoke of her grandmother.

"She had special gifts given to her by the gods. She used those gifts to help her people; she gave us warnings; she gave us healings; she gave us comfort." Iyannah felt the tears trickle down her cheeks. Many others were also in tears. But

Iyannah's tears were not of grief; rather they were tears of emotion and pride at the moving tributes now being paid to her grandmother.

The Story-teller sat down seemingly well-pleased at the effect his words had produced. Others now stood up in turn to add their more personal anecdotes. Even-tide approached and the drum began again; the mourners embraced the family once more, and the procession departed.

Iyannah was exhausted. She helped Aunt Mila clear away, and she swept the outer area of their home. More water would be needed, but it would have to wait until morning.

Iyannah needed to sleep.

Chapter 7

Iyannah's week passed in serving and fetching, and listening to repeated reminiscences. She saw Dani only fleetingly, when she somehow managed to time her visits to the brook to coincide with his return from the sea. There was little Dani could do to help her. She was so weary, but now that Spring had finally arrived she knew Dani, too, had much to do. The gradually lengthening hours of daylight meant much work had to be done on the boats after the inactivity of the winter months.

The lamenting procession returned on the last night of mourning to escort her grandmother's body to the high place near the moors. The Lamenters had drums and shakers and rattling instruments to frighten off evil spirits and also to make noises of celebration as her grandmother departed to the place of Eternal Feasting. Iyannah's family followed behind and others came after. Many were carrying torches to light the way to the Otherworld.

Iyannah walked slowly behind her mother and father. As they began to climb upwards, Dani appeared beside her. She was grateful to lean on his arm, and she no longer felt so alone.

The final rites were completed and torches thrown onto the funeral pyre. As the flames leaped upwards, Dani drew a distressed Iyannah away. The people began to disperse back to their own homes and Iyannah and Dani walked to the cliff edge and looked at the sea. The wind was rushing across the wild moor land; yet the sea seemed calm. They were above the most dangerous rocks of the bay.

"Listen," said Dani.

Iyannah heard a low rumbling noise that seemed to come from under the ground. It sounded like thunder rising from below!

"What is it, Dani? Is it an earthquake?"

(Iyannah hoped it was not a sign from the gods. Nor from her grandmother!)

"No," said Dani, "it is stranger than that. Below us is a cave, I have been there before. When the tide begins to change stones inside the cave move and rumble. And the cave walls make the sound echo even louder. Listen carefully."

Sure enough, the sound did keep pace with the waves as they came ashore and withdrew.

Iyannah's eyes were widening in wonder.

Dani laughed, "I'll take you there, one day," he promised.

Iyannah was not sure she wanted to go anywhere near such a place. But, at least, Dani wanted to see her again, and that was what she wanted, too.

Chapter 8

Danni set out in his small boat very early the next morning. The sea was like a lake, scarcely a ripple breaking the surface. The other small boats, his two brothers in their boats among them, headed south from the bay thus avoiding the jagged rocks of the coast that lay to the north. But Dani was in adventurous mood. It was a perfect day for exploring and the kinder weather offered a rare chance to travel further north than ever before. His brothers shook their heads as he left. Dani, the youngest in the family, was always off on his own. How many times had they had to go to his aid? They were the responsible ones. Dani had been blessed (or cursed) with a different approach to life.

There was very little breeze so once clear of the rocks and out at sea, Dani sat back content to drift wherever his boat would take him although keeping a reasonably central course away from the rocky shoreline. Dani knew only too well that menacing currents could draw him and his boat ever nearer to their destructive forces.

Dani was now able to observe from safe distance the land that lay to his left. He was looking for signs of other tribal occupation but saw none. High steep cliffs rose straight from the sea's level and there were no hospitable bays affording the access that there was at Craghburn.

This was the life he loved: alone with the sea, the sky above and a feeling of peace in his soul. He thought of Iyannah and his plans for them to be together. He had known Iyannah all his life. She was younger than he was and yet it seemed that she had always been there. She truly was his soul-mate. He pictured her in his mind: a tall, but slight figure with brown hair shot through with golden lights. She always wore her long, fine hair neatly braided into the curve of her neck. She had so much grace about her every movement, her hands emphasising her words as she spoke; and her footsteps light and dainty as she walked by his side. But it was her eyes that fascinated him. They were hazel, yet flecked with gold like her hair, and those eyes so clearly reflected her every thought and emotion. They were indeed a mirror to her inner soul, burning darkest amber in times of distress and yet seeming as pale as sunlight in early summer when she was at her happiest.

But it wasn't merely her grace and beauty that had attracted Dani to her. Iyannah always understood him. She listened intently to his wilder schemes and supported all his plans. To her he was already a hero; and soon others would recognise him as a great adventurer!

Chapter 9

The summer that eventually came was unsettled. Stifling heat often gave way to thunder storms. Sometimes it seemed that steam was rising from the very sands. But Iyannah walked often with Dani and her grandmother was always in her thoughts.

"You see that white flower", she would hear herself say, "you use only the petals. It makes a sweet calming drink. And that red one is for aches and pains. I give it to my father sometimes."

She had learned so much from her grandmother without even realising it. Maybe that was the true legacy she had meant to give her.

Dani was listening attentively, so she continued.

"And that one, we use the root from it. If you dry it and grind it to a powder, it makes….. a love potion!"

Dani was quick to reply.

"You don't need that then, Iyannah, for I love you already."

Dani had plans for them to be together but Iyannah was not so sure. It wasn't that she didn't love Dani, for she did, but life among the 'fisher-folk' as her mother called them, was very different from life with her family.

Her first visit to Dani's home had been far from reassuring.

Where he lived the houses were built perilously close to the cliff's edge and also close to the wild moor lands. The houses were small and very close together in almost a separate enclave. The smell of fish was bad enough but the smell of the wood tar used to paint over the boats was all-pervading.

29

Dani's mother was struggling up the steep slope with a huge basket of fish on her back. She had carried it up from the water's edge.

"So you're Iyannah", she said when she had breath to speak. "I would hardly have known you. The last time I saw you, you were so shy you hid behind your mother's skirts. Come inside and let me look at you." She put down her heavy basket. Iyannah could feel herself blushing, but Dani behind her made sure she went in.

A cooling drink was poured for them all and then Dani's mother began to talk. "Two boats not back yet, Dani. These storms are not good. The Sea-god is angry."

She began to relate to Iyannah frightening tales of the Sea-god and his sons who could take on animal or even human shapes to look for those they wished to invite to their kingdom beneath the waves.

"There's great palaces under the sea and nearly everyone I know has lost some-one to the Sea-god," she warned by raising her index finger.

Iyannah turned scared eyes to Dani who tried to change the flow of conversation. "Where's Father tonight?" asked Dani.

"I thought you'd know," she said looking at Iyannah. Iyannah had no idea what she meant.

"He's up at the pastures with your Dad. Something about making wooden pipes of elm tree to let the water flow to all the fields. Been there since early afternoon, too." Iyannah and Dani exchanged glances. Her father and Dani's? That was unexpected.

As the chat continued it did seem to Iyannah that Dani was his mother's favourite. His two brothers were the ones who went to the trading posts to sell the day's catch whilst Dani helped in the boatyard and nearer to the house. And if he sailed back late, from one of his adventures, then food was ready for him whenever he returned.

The money brought in by the selling of the fish was little enough, and poor recompense for the dangers faced catching it. The boatyard did not fare much better. Few could afford new boats and Dani spent most of his time repairing older ones. Iyannah tried to take in every word and wondered how on earth she and Dani could ever make a life together.

And there was another problem. Many of their people had begun to embrace Christianity; some had even moved to communities around the monasteries that had been set up. Rebirth, and even resurrection, was acceptable to the Celtic mind and the communal way of life of the early Church was easily comparable to the life they already shared. But it took an even greater 'leap of faith' to abandon completely the gods who had always protected them. Great reliance rested on the stories and histories that had been handed down to them by their ancestors. Iyannah would never give up her beliefs that had been so impressed upon her by her grandmother.

But she knew that Dani was intrigued to learn of a Saviour who made the fishermen

His closest friends. And that worried her.

Perhaps it was because of these doubts and fears, but Iyannah now began to have strange dreams; dreams that disturbed her greatly. She tried to ignore them. She no longer wanted to be like her grandmother; she only wanted to 'see' a bright future and not to receive signs and warnings.

Chapter 10

Pale moonlight sent tantalising glimmers of light dancing on the evening tidal waters. Iyannah and Dani walked along the shore-line circling towards the southern curve of the bay. Together the climbed the Faerie Steps as these rocks were known, and carefully stepped over slippery patches of moss-green seaweed. Shallow pools of crystal-clear water offered homes to many pink and red starfish and sea anemones too. Tiny crabs scuttled across from one small pool to another and hermit crabs hastened to find empty shells for sanctuary. Limpets holding on tightly to the flat rock surfaces shone white in the moonlight and occasionally black branches of seaweed crackled under their feet.

Dani picked up a pure white shell, perfectly spiralled with purple-pink pearl cocooned round and round inside it. He offered it to Iyannah. But Iyannah's eyes were dark and troubled and she did not speak.

"What is bothering you, Iya? he asked in exasperation. "Have I upset you? You are so quiet, today."

Iyannah knew she had to tell him.

"No, Dani, I am not upset. I always want to be with you. You know that." "Then tell me what is worrying you?"

Iyannah sighed, and sat down on one of the larger white rocks and looked up at him. "I don't know how we can make a life together, Dani."

Dani seemed relieved as he sat down beside her. He put his arm protectingly around her.

"Don't you think I know your fears", he laughed.

"I saw how it was when my mother spoke of the Sea-god and his sons. And I know the life for a fisherman's wife is one of worrying and waiting, and constant dread."

"I do worry, Dani, I worry so much every time you set out. I worry when I see the big waves come rolling in and the skies growing darker. And the rocks out there!"

She shook her head.

"Don't worry about the rocks. I know every part of this shore. And I know the moods of the sea. But I am not always going to do this; I want more for us, Iyannah."

Iyannah was taken aback. Dani seemed to understand her so well and as she listened it was as if a huge weight had been lifted from her heart.

"I love the sea, it's true, but I have better plans for you and me," Dani continued.

"I have spoken to my father. He is going to help me build a small flat boat to go on the river, not the sea. Each season we dry fish and seaweed to save for the winter. And other people need this food too. If I catch enough fish to dry, then I can go by river to sell them to other settlements. It will be easier than travelling to the trading posts by cart in the winter months".

Iyannah listened attentively; it was a new idea and it sounded good.

"And," he added persuasively, "if you collect and dry your herbs, I will sell them, too. And one day we will have enough to leave Craghburn and move to a bigger place altogether. Why not?"

Iyannah was horrified.

"Leave Craghburn? I never thought of doing that!"

"Well, maybe not", Dani retracted quickly, "but we could build a house further away, by the river, or near the woods, if you like."

"And maybe in time", agreed Iyannah, "you won't need to go and catch the fish, only sell the dry fish that are surplus from others. We could make it work, I am sure."

Iyannah was filled with relief and excitement. Dani was right; the time had come for communities to trade more readily together. A new age was coming.

Iyannah's eyes sparkled as she made her way homewards. Dani understood her so well; her worries and fears were gone. They would have a good life together.

Near her home, she took up a small stone and drew a circle in the soft earth. Inside the circle she outlined two figures: her and Dani. The circle would keep them together always and protect them from outside harm. And in the centre she laid the pure white shell.

Dani, however, was thinking that if he could just discover the feeding grounds to the north used by the shoals of small fish that he often saw, then he would have plenty of fish to dry and sell. That would have to be accomplished first.

Chapter 11

Iyannah stood at the top of the highest sand dune. Sharp grasses and particles of sand encroached into her soft sandals as she gazed down to the shore.

"If it wasn't for you, I'd be down there", she softly chided the young boy in her arms.

He wriggled wanting to be down on the grass.

There were no small boats to be seen; the young men had left early and would not be back until dusk. A group of women were on the flat rocks at the south side of the curve of the bay, her mother among them. They were collecting shell-fish, an extra treat for tonight's meal! A few older boys were at the water's edge, taking it in turn to skim stones across the tranquil sea. Younger children were playing on the wet sand, and sometimes bravely approached the water's edge only to run back as the waves raced to meet them. Iyannah could hear the sounds of their laughter even from her place so high above them. The rocks to the northern side were sharp and narrow forever pointing towards the sea.

It would soon be August. The summer solstice was over and the last festival before the winter was due to be held on the first of August: the Festival of Light. And this year it would be even more joyous. Iyannah had a secret: she would be one of the young people entering into 'handfastings' or 'trial marriages' that would last a year and a day. She knew in her heart that she and Dani would be together forever and that they would return the following year to make their contract to each other a permanent one. Of that she was certain.

It was a beautiful golden day. The sea sparkled in the sunlight, its white foam lace- edging the darker wet sand. This sand in response reflected back the warmth of the sun. The dry sand was white-gold with pearly shells dotted upon it and swathes of seaweed, of green, brown and red, linked their long branches along the high-water mark.

Iyannah so wished that she could join her people there on the beach but she had a duty to take care of Bren, her young brother. Soon her mother would be back and she would be free to go down and watch for Dani's small boat returning. She held Bren tightly and reluctantly made her way homewards.

She went inside and set Bren down in his wooden cradle. A pot of water would need to be ready for the collected shellfish but today these would be cooked in the large communal pot in the open space just beyond the houses. It was too warm for indoor fires to be lit.

Bren began to cry. He was almost too big for his cradle now. Fair haired and rosy cheeked, he was growing into a fine boy. She rocked the cradle gently and sang to him softly. It was a lullaby that her grandmother had sung to her. She greatly missed her grandmother.

Grandmother always swore to the existence of the Little People who delighted in playing tricks on humankind.

"No young baby should ever be left unattended lest the Faery Folk take the child in envy and leave behind a changeling", were her oft-repeated words to young Iyannah.

Bren was sleeping now. Iyannah rolled up the mats that served for beds and stored them in the alcove cupboard cut into the stone wall. She ate a little of the round flat bread that her mother had baked on the hot stone oven outside their house before leaving to gather shellfish. Long strips of seaweed hung at the side of the opening to their home, strung there to dry in the summer sun, which had now reached its highest point.

"I wonder where Dani is now", she thought.

Shortly after noon, Iyannah mother returned. And so did her father! Usually he spent all day in the growing fields, but the day was exceptionally hot. He wanted to rest, preferring to work later into the long summer's evening.

With the help of Dani's father, (the master boat-builder), he had devised a system of watering through carved-out wooden elm channels so that each and every plant was given the best encouragement to grow well. To Iyannah's mother, Jalb was an ideal husband: he was a good provider and that was all that mattered.

Iyannah greeted both her parents and set out bread for them to eat. There was also soft cheese and small oatcakes that had been baked on the griddle: her father's favourite! Bren was lifted from his cradle to sit with his father. Iyannah poured water for them to drink and then sat with them around the low wooden table.

"Did you see Dani this morning, Mama?" she asked.

"No", came the reply. "He must have left very early. I saw some of the boats go out, but not Dani's."

"Dani the Dreamer, you mean," teased her father. "Always off somewhere when there is work to be done!"

Iyannah's eyes darkened.

"He works hard enough in the evenings, repairing boats and building new ones", she retorted defensively.

"He doesn't catch that many fish though, does he?" Her mother intervened to end this banter:

"We'll be needing more water for tonight." "I'll walk back with you, father", said Iyannah.

She liked to visit the brook and the sacred spring nearby, and was well-used to carrying the earthenware pitcher.

"And we'll need plenty of fresh herbs, too, for the shellfish pot."

Chapter 12

Iyannah waved to her father as he returned to the pastures, and she climbed the steep path from the lower hillside. The air was sweet with the scent of blossom; there would be plenty of berries soon. The grass on these slopes was soft underfoot and she treaded lightly enjoying the sensations around her of Nature at its summer best. The woods would soon be offering their store of provisions for those who sought them. As well as berries, the hazel nuts were green and velvety and ready for further ripening before the autumnal equinox. There would be a good harvest this year, for sure.

She reached the brook quickly and set down her jug. Then she went as always to pay homage to the Sacred Spring, offering a prayer of thanksgiving to the god of the Hills. Then she went back to the brook and filled the water-carrier before turning to go back down the woodland path.

A sudden rustling in the bushes beyond startled her. Then came snuffling noises and strange squeals as the undergrowth seemed to move. She stood still in terror, her grandmother's wilder stories pulsating through her head. A wild animal? Or a monster with great eyes that blazed? A hobgoblin? Or maybe one from the strange tribes that some said resided up in the cold bleak hill-tops. Perhaps she had unwittingly offended the god of the Hills? She forced open her eyes that had closed in panic.

Then she laughed out loud.

A tiny wild pig, a mere piglet, scuttled across on short stubby legs. She saw the little curled tail disappear into the thicket.

But just as suddenly came back her grandmother's warning: the gods take many shapes. You must heed their warnings. And hadn't Grandmother many a tale of the dire consequences that befell those who did not respect the signs. Worse still, the pig was the symbolic animal for Manannan, son of the Sea-god! All sailors were reluctant to sail at the very mention of the word 'pig' in their presence for fear Manannan would send his great waves to take them down to his abode?

Over the highest hill a dark cloud appeared, hovered and suddenly settled. Iyannah felt a deep sense of fore-boding and thought fearfully of Dani. What did these signs mean?

Her grandmother would have known.

Chapter 13

Dani's voyage was going well. The high cliffs appeared inhabited only by seabirds. He watched in awe as they swooped down and dived, then rose with fish trapped in their sharp beaks. Some of these birds were graceful in flight and expert divers; others seemed almost comical, with their shorter but more colourful beaks and extravagant splashings as they struggled with their prey. But they all seemed to find food in plenty. The ocean was boundless in its provision. Dani hoped that one day he would somehow outwit and catch a great fish to take home to his people for feasting! Then he too would become one of the heroes, like those of old.

Just then he felt his boat rock unsteadily. Maybe a big fish was already underneath it! But what he did see was more incredible: a huge shoal of silver fish. He marvelled at the sight. There must be hundreds of them, he thought, and they were moving rapidly northwards. He leaned flat in his boat and used his hands as paddles to follow this amazing sight. By lifting only his head he could watch their ever swifter journey, as they cut effortlessly through the water.

It took only a short while for Dani to realise that he had no need to paddle. His boat was moving along with the fish at the same speed and to the same purpose. Where were they all heading? Everything was happening in a fleeting instant, but to Dani it seemed that Time itself had ceased to exist. He seemed almost to become detached as though he was somehow looking down on the drama unfolding, without being a part of it.

Dani, boat and fish hurtled faster and faster and Dani saw ahead the coming climax to their journey. His hands now gripped the sides of his boat as he desperately tried to stay on board. The silver fish were being drawn into whirling circles that rippled and glittered in a blur of light. Faster and faster these little fish swirled as Dani gazed in fascination. He felt giddiness overpower him even as he watched them. The sacred rowan branch given to him by Iyannah dislodged itself from the prow of his boat and seemed to stay suspended in mid-air, motionless, before plunging into the abyss that had now opened in the midst of the sea. The fish were still circling ever downwards and Dani knew he and his boat were fated to follow. Perhaps the mighty god of the Sea was summoning him; perhaps this was to be his greatest adventure. He was not afraid. But what would Iyannah say when he told her about it?

Then all he could feel was falling, falling, as the boat dropped down into the gaping hole in the deep ocean. And he too whirled downwards, blinded by silver lights and no longer able to breathe.

Chapter 14

Iyannah sat very still on the grass and tried to think more clearly. The image of a pig's face was indeed symbolic of the Sea-god. But she was not going out on the sea. That was Dani's province. She much preferred the woodland and the pastureland. If Dani had seen the piglet he would not have gone out in his boat that morning; but he had not seen it! And the dark cloud on the high hill was not so very unusual; weren't clouds always collecting over the hills even in summer?

And yet a great fear still gripped her. Something was not right, she could feel it, sense it, and even smell it; disaster loomed. A kind of suffocation consumed her. Her breathing was rapid and her heart was pounding. What could this mean? Was it a premonition like those that her grandmother had so often experienced?

She pictured her grandmother as though reaching out to her for advice. The images that came were unsettling. Strange it was then, how clearly her Grandmother's words had stayed with her, as though past conversations had been stored all the while in her head; Grandma's tales and wisdom were the legacy that had been left to her.

It was Dani alone who had seen her grief at losing her grandmother. He had offered her comfort and tried to share her burden. He had been there to listen to her when others were too busy themselves to notice her suffering. Without Dani, she would have been lost. She begged all of the gods and all of the heroes of the past to save Dani from harm and bring him safely back to her. But for once, these prayers brought little comfort. In her heart a deep darkness persisted.

Somehow she managed to take the water to her waiting mother and was duly scolded for not bringing any herbs.

Then Iyannah made her way to the shoreline.

Chapter 15

"Iya, Iya" came a loud scream.

Iyannah awoke to find herself still on the beach. She had sat there, a lonely figure with her knees bent up under her loose tunic and her head resting on them, all night. From time to time, she had lifted her head and sought in vain to see Dani's boat come into view. But it was not so. His brothers had returned late into the evening, and reassured her that the sea was calm and that Dani would be safe. They would set out the next morning and find him. They did not tell her that Dani had sailed far to the North.

The sun was only just rising above the horizon far over the sea. The cries came again: "Iya, Iya", but it was the sound of a hungry seagull seeking an early breakfast. Her limbs ached, but not as deeply as did her heart. She struggled to stand and scanned the ocean again. There was nothing to see for miles and miles. Even the sun-god seemed to mock her as he sent his earliest rays filtering over the water directly towards her.

Dani's brothers returned to the beach with Dani's father and a large boat which they were preparing to launch. Iyannah begged to go with them but they would not take her. Other smaller boats were now setting off anxious to help in the search for Dani. Groups of womenfolk came to join Iyannah but she was oblivious to their solicitudes. How could any of them know how she felt?

A strange hush had fallen over the whole community. Dani's mother waited at home, and some of the women went to be with her. Children were called back from their usual play to go with them; other women reluctantly left Iyannah and returned to the everyday tasks that had to be done. Food was brought for Iyannah by her mother, but she did not eat. That evening brought no news. Iyannah remained leaning against a rock, a soft shawl now wrapped around her shoulders by some kind soul who could think of no other way to offer comfort to the distraught young girl.

The following day came and went. But by evening Dani's father approached Iyannah. She knew by his slow walk and hunched shoulders that he was bringing the news that she dreaded. She had no need to look at his face.

"We've found him, Iyannah", he said softly.

"His body was washed up onto the rocks at the northernmost point. We found no trace of his boat."

Iyannah clutched her throat. Her grief rose to choke her. She tried to speak, but no words came. Dani's father stepped forward to console her, but she raised her hand to stop him. She wanted no-one close to her, except Dani, and that could never be.

Instead Iyannah walked past Dani's father, and somehow found the strength to climb up away from the beach. She grasped clumps of the spiky grasses and pulled herself to the top of the dunes. But she did not go home. She moved steadily as though in a trance, beyond the settlement, beyond the fields and beyond the spring. Higher and higher she climbed from the foothills and there she found a small cave, half-hidden by trees and bushes. She threw herself down onto the cold floor and poured out her grief in sobs that echoed from every wall of the cave.

How could she celebrate the Festival of Light? It held no meaning.

For her world was in total darkness.

PART TWO

Chapter 16

Joja clutched her mother's hand tightly. She was very frightened of the approaching dark hooded figures and the accompanying low drum beat. The crowd of people around her were strangely silent as the procession reached them. Her mother tried to reassure her.

"Look, that's Brother Bartram at the front. See he carries the golden cross," she whispered.

Joja watched closely.

Behind Brother Bartram, other monks walked solemnly carrying various handmade artefacts to depict the story of the birth of Christendom to their followers.

"That's the cockerel that crowed when Peter betrayed our Master," her mother pointed out.

Joja saw the tears in her mother's eyes as the monks moved slowly on: one carrying a long whip; another holding a mallet and nails; and then a monk who was bearing a long spear. Joja did not understand any of it but she knew it was greatly affecting those around her. They bowed their heads in silence as each item passed by. A monk in a brown robe came next, holding aloft a long stick with a crown of thorns upon it. Sobs came from a woman standing near to her, and tears streamed down her mother's face. Three crosses came next, the largest one in the middle; and then an image of the Risen Christ wearing a golden crown. Relief came to the crowd as the resurrection was thus marked out before them.

As the solemn procession ended the crowd, as one, moved slowly behind the monks and followed them towards the sea. It had been perfectly timed. The causeway was wide and open: the monks could safely return to Lindisfarne before the tide encroached on their pathway. Soon they would be back on their island retreat and cut off from the mainland once more.

Joja's mother had found solace for herself in her religion and she had hopes that Joja would become similarly enlightened and find acceptance into the new and growing Christian community. But then Joja had always been a difficult child.

"When you were born you screamed and screamed for three months," her mother constantly exclaimed.

Joja's early tantrums had been a sore trial but whilst her mother had been very patient, others were quick to suggest that this child must be 'possessed of demons'. Joja's step-father already had three sons when he had married her mother. It was a necessary marriage: his first wife had died young and left him with little choice but to find another woman to look after his young boys. And as he took on Joja in return, her mother was very grateful to him. In truth he was old enough to be Joja's grandfather and he found Joja less and less agreeable as she (and he) grew older. He had little, or no, affection for her, and found it easier to keep companionship with his own growing sons. Joja soon learned that nothing she did was ever pleasing to him, so she had given up even trying. Joja knew nothing of her 'real' father. No-one spoke of him and her mother only shook her head and sighed if Joja tried to question her.

Joja's red hair was thick and curled outward no matter how much she combed it. She had broken many a fishbone comb trying to straighten it; nothing seemed to work!

She always looked unkempt, not neatly braided like the other young girls. She watched despairingly as her mother slaved from early morning to late evening for her husband and his sons and vowed that this was not the kind of life she would ever want. It was doubtful that young Joja would ever find a husband who'd cope with her disrespectful outbursts; she did not even have many friends. Most of the children of her age avoided her: she was 'different' and not one of them.

"One day," she thought, "I will leave this place forever!"

Her mother, a 'Christ-follower' tried very hard to understand her daughter, and hoped that Joja would reach adolescence with some acceptance of her lot in life. But so far, Joja seemed to reject any good advice and continued to be wilful and resentful of any restraints placed on her. She had been warned many times not to venture on to the wild moors that lay beyond the settlement, but this was the place that Joja loved best!

"You must not go there," her mother emphasised repeatedly.

"There are dangerous snakes there; and great bogs that can swallow up a horse and cart and many people in an instance. Bad spirits lurk there. And wild beasts. Do not wander away from the pastures. Great harm could come to you."

But the wildness of the moor held too much attraction for Joja. Here she could be totally alone. She would lie on a bed of heather she'd found that was shaped exactly to her size and gaze up at the clouds and listen to the wind and the waves. And she wondered if indeed there was a single god above it all: a god who looked after everyone, but not her, it seemed!

And now she was late and her mother would be so cross. Again!

Chapter 17

Joja looked down towards the flat rocks. Streng had called a meeting and everyone was gathering there. She could see her mother beckoning her to come quickly. No doubt her mother would be agitated that Joja had not gone down with her and the rest of the community.

With a deep sigh, she now slid rapidly down the sand dune and raced across to join her mother who was sitting on one of the wooden benches that had been set out on the flattest area of rock. Streng stood alone in front of the assembled community.

Streng the Elder, as he was known, was not from their settlement. His family had converted to Christianity upon the first visit of Cuthbert to their settlement in the far north of Scotland. Cuthbert had travelled by donkey long ago, seeking to bring Christian beliefs to such small separate communities. Upon Cuthbert's later retreat to the island of Lindisfarne, families like that of Streng had followed and set up their own community on the mainland. A monastery had been built on Lindisfarne, an ideal setting for meditation and seclusion. Like Cuthbert before him, Streng tried to explain that the new Christians must abandon their old beliefs. The elder people respected the new religion greatly, but still revered old superstitions and passed these down as advice to the young.

Streng was intense and deeply dedicated to bringing a stronger spirituality to the more remote areas. He had visited Craghburn several times but the people seemed to have little inclination to change their old ways and, unlike Streng, they did not feel the urgency that the return of the Messiah could be imminent.

His opening prayer was to seek to reassure the people before him:

'Let nothing disturb thee, nothing afright thee; all things are passing. God never changes! Patient endurance attains to all things;

Who God possesses in nothing is wanting; alone God suffices' Amen.

Streng then praised the community spirit that he had found in evidence in Craghburn.

'You help each other in difficult times; food is shared amongst you. All of you work equally hard according to your talents.'

The community relaxed and some even smiled.

'But' he went on, 'I need again to remind you that God alone is the Creator of all things. Why therefore do some of you consider a tree to be worthy of worship? Why do you consider a well, or a spring to be venerated? God created every element of creation and it is to God alone that we should give thanks. It is He who provides for our needs.'

He paused and gazed closely at the people in front of him. His eyes were blazing from below thick black eyebrows, and his small straggly grey beard gave him the appearance of an Old Testament prophet. His voice was stern and his words emphatic.

'I see some amongst you wearing small twigs of holly to ward off ill-feeling from others! You place your faith in a sprig from a tree, a tree given to you by the Creator! For shame!'

He mocked them for they much revered all trees and gave to each one a designation of protection. It had long been thought that the trees themselves were their ancestors; and did not all their sustenance come from trees: food; fire; wood for boats and ploughs; tools and weapons; and their earliest houses? Several in the gathered assembly were discomfited by his words; others saw no harm in keeping tradition whilst also accepting Christ as an example of wisdom and love. Many found it only too easy to equate the two.

Streng was not finished:

'I have heard that some amongst you visit the Wise Woman of the Hill in times of trouble! You ask her to lift imagined curses; offer healing potions; to interpret dreams and signs for you! This is not the way you should be following.'

Joja was intrigued. She had never heard tell of such a woman, but it was obvious that many others had. They shuffled uncomfortably on the small benches, looking down at the grey rock beneath their feet.

Streng spoke now more gently, seeking to inspire a deeper faith that would enable these people to leave behind the ways of the past which held such sway upon them.

'Christ is the Way, the Truth and the Light', he emphasised and lifted his hands above the people.

'Let Him not return and find this community wanting. God bless and keep you.'

He offered a blessing and the response 'Amen' came from the people, who it must be said, were quite shaken by Streng's strong words to them.

For once, Joja walked back up with her mother. A rough but firmer path to the left of the sand dunes offered easier ascent to the more elderly. Joja's thoughts, however, were not spiritual. She was trying to imagine this Wise Woman. Who was she? What strange powers might she possess?

An old lady walked alongside them.

'Did you ever visit the Wise Woman?' she asked Joja's mother.

Joja's mother did not answer, but the older woman continued the conversation anyway.

'I went to her when I was cursed with pains in my fingers. She was kindness itself, and her herbs helped me. I would not have been able to work but for her!'

Others were quick to add their personal anecdotes.

'My daughter went to see her before she got married. And good advice she gave her. We knew he was not right for her, but did she listen to us! The Wise Woman read the signs for her, and she came back and married Agmann instead!'

'He's a good man is Agmann. Your daughter did well to heed the signs.'

'She makes offerings to the Hill and River gods, and we never want for fresh water. We have had good supplies all these years.'

'Streng does not know our ways. He is not of our people'.

Joja feigned disinterest, but her heart was beating rapidly. She must find a way to meet this Wise Woman.

Chapter 18

It had been a dismal day. Swirling fog moved in from the sea bringing cold air and dampness to everything. Joja's mother struggled to light the fire inside their home and the smoky fumes blew inwards instead of out through the opening above.

"Joja, we need more water, before father comes back. Be quick, now."

Joja wrapped her long cloak around her and took up the large water jug. She climbed easily upwards to the water inlet that brought a steady supply of sweet water down from the hills to the settlement. In her eagerness, she filled the tall jug to the brim making it almost too heavy for her to carry. She struggled valiantly to carry it homewards, but alas, and so nearly home, her foot slipped on the wet grass. It was enough to send Joja and her jug sprawling: the water was gone and Joja's knee was grazed.

"Oh, why does this have to happen to me?" she groaned.

She debated whether to go home and tell her mother about her mishap, or just go back and fetch more water.

But before she could decide, her mother rushed out of the small house obviously looking for her.

"Where is that water? Father is here now and I cannot cook without it!"

Joja held out the empty jug and tried to explain. But it seemed no-one had time to listen. Her step-father appeared at the entrance door and he was angry.

"Why am I cursed with such a stupid girl?" he shouted, glaring at her mother. He swung his hand to strike Joja, but she was too nimble for him. She darted behind her mother as he fought to keep his balance.

"When I catch hold of you, I will give you such a beating as you'll never forget!" he yelled in frustration. He tried to push her mother out of the way.

Joja turned and ran, leaving the jug on the grass. She ran on and on, towards the moors, as far away as possible from that man in his fury.

When Joja finally stopped running, she was further into the moor lands than she had ever reached before. The fog was much thicker here and clung steadfastly to the ground. She could see little in front of her, and even less behind the way she had come. She spread out her cape and sat down on it. Bitter tears of self-pity welled up in her eyes and she shook with rage and fear. She gripped her hands together in anguish. What could she do now? If she went back, he would be waiting for her. If she went further, she might fall into the awful bogs her mother had told her about. Soon it would be dark, and then the moors would be even more frightening; she would never find her way out.

She lay down, resting her head on her hands and tried to calm her wretched thoughts.

How long she lay there she had no idea; maybe she had even slept from sheer exhaustion after such emotional torment. But now strange noises carried through the fog that caused her great terror: loud echoes of words she could not understand; heavy drum beats and rhythmic splashing sounds. Maybe it was only in her head. Was she imagining her stepfather chasing after her; or maybe his sons beating the bushes to find her? But no, these sounds were coming from the direction of the sea. She edged nearer very cautiously and then she saw it!

A huge head suspended in the sky; a head that bobbed up and down in time to the sound of the waves and the shouting. This was no human head. It had great jaws and protruding eyes and a writhing long neck that disappeared into the depth of the mists. Joja knew what it was: it was a dragon! And it was moving towards Craghburn. And dragons meant fire and scorched earth and destruction.

She had to go back and warn her people.

Chapter 19

It was almost daylight when poor Joja, wet and bedraggled, finally found her way back to the settlement. Her face was pale and tearstained and she was still in great fear of her stepfather. But maybe he would forgive her when she told him of the dragon; he would be able to warn the others and save them all from the worst ravages that a dragon could bring. At least that was her hope.

The door partition to her home had been moved and the entrance was open. Her mother must be awake. Joja drew nearer as silently as she could.

"Oh, my poor child! Come and take off your wet clothes and lay them around the hearth. I will get your some herb tea or you will suffer a fever. Where have you been? I was so worried all night!"

Joja looked around her anxiously.

"Your stepfather went out early. He has taken his sons over the hills to snare wild fowl. They should be gone for three days or more."

"But, Mama, I have to warn him." Joja hugged her mother and sobbed in fear. "A dragon is coming!"

"A dragon! Whatever are you talking about?"

"I saw it over the sea and it is coming to Craghburn!" "Calm down, Joja. And tell me properly."

Joja confessed to her mother that she had run away on to the moor. Her mother listened quietly but was not best pleased with her errant young daughter.

"How many times have I told you always to be truthful, Joja? If you think this story of a dragon will protect you from the upset you have caused this family, it will not work! No-one has seen a dragon for more than two hundred years! And why should one suddenly appear to you and bring harm to Craghburn? Stop all this nonsense!"

But Joja insisted that her story was true and would not be persuaded otherwise.

Her mother sighed and gave her the soothing tea to drink, hoping that it would help to pacify the agitated young girl.

"If you do not believe me, Mama, then I have to tell the others. I have to warn them. I know the stories of our ancestors; I know about dragons. They breathe fire and destroy the crops and burn the land. You must let me warn our neighbours."

"Hush, Joja, rest now. You can tell them later." Her mother did not know what else to say.

The warmth of the fire, and the comfort of her mother, lulled Joja into a fitful sleep. She stirred often, and screamed out several times. Her mother was sure that she had indeed caught a fever and fetched a cloth soaked in cool water to place on her brow.

By afternoon Joja sat up suddenly.

"The dragon, Mama. It will be here soon. What are we going to do?"

And despite her Christian beliefs, Joja's mother could think of only one answer; go and ask for help from the Wise Woman.

Chapter 20

Joja and her mother set off early the next day. Her mother was anxious that others should not see them and guess where they were going. Together they passed through the part of the farmland known as Old Jalb's fields. The fog had lifted and a pale sun was beaming down making it into a mild autumn morning.

Joja was curious as to how her mother knew where to seek out the mysterious Wise Woman of the Hill, but she did not ask. She busied herself collecting blackberries and found some ripened hazel nuts too. The air smelt good and sweet and it was a pleasure to be out on the hillside before winter's approach.

Her mother was puffing at the uphill climb. It was getting warmer as the sun rose higher.

"I'm going ahead," said Joja, "I'm going to wash my hands in the brook."

Joja reached the brook easily and began to wash her blackberry stained hands. She was so intent on this task, that she did not see a figure emerge and move slowly towards the once-sacred spring. But the sound of mumbled soft words reached her ears. A woman was beside the spring, and was praying audibly to the god of the Hills. Scarlet berries were already bright on the rowan tree by her side. Joja stood silent and still as the woman laid an offering on the large flat stone which lay partly over the gushing spring. Her offering was a twisted, plaited circle of flowers, leaves and cornstalks, intricately woven together. Joja felt that she should speak but did not wish to startle this stranger so intent at her devotions.

But before Joja could gather her thoughts, the woman turned and gazed directly at her. The woman smiled and nodded but did not speak, as though she was waiting for Joja to address her.

"I'm sorry if I disturbed you," said Joja in a half-whisper.

The figure before her wore a long grey dress. A white scarf fell loosely over white hair that gleamed with silvery lights in the soft sunlight. Her eyes seemed to hold deep sadness in them; she appeared almost detached from her surroundings as she moved gracefully towards Joja.

Joja felt more than a little afraid, yet in the same instant realisation came to her - this must be her!

"You came looking for me," said the woman. "You seek my help?"

Joja's mother had now reached the brook. She went forward to embrace the woman in grey and it was obvious to Joja that the two of them must have been well-acquainted at some time in the past.

"This is my daughter, Joja," introduced her mother. "I would be grateful if you could listen to her and advise her."

The woman beckoned Joja to follow her, and her mother nodded.

"You go, Joja. I will rest here by the brook till you return. But mind you tell only the truth!"

Chapter 21

Joja followed the woman who was signalling that she do so. Upwards from the spring, the foothills lost their smoothness and became crags of white stone with grey-green mosses and small white flowerets clinging desperately to them. These plants seem strange to Joja. They were not like the soft blues and greens of the woodlands; nor were they like the tall sharp grasses of the dunes where occasional sea-daisies lay scattered; nor even like the purple-pink heather that spread for miles across the moors. The landscape here was much bleaker and harsher. And much further from home!

Between some small whitened shrubs a narrow path now led. And there, at the end, surprisingly, was a garden of herbs neatly laid out row by row. Sloped behind this garden was a shallow cave. Grass above formed a 'roof' to this hidden dwelling.

'Come in, now, Joja, and talk for a while. I sense you are troubled and I will help you if I can'

The Wise Woman pulled back a loosely woven trellis of willow twigs that served as a door and Joja went inside.

A small fire burned in the centre of the cave. White stones made the hearth that surrounded it. Many candles were set out in natural alcoves formed in the rock and sturdy rush mats were strewn on the floor. Bunches of drying herbs were hung on snippets of twine between some of the crevices in the cave-walls so it smelt sweet and fresh inside, not dark and dank as Joja had expected. It was a warm and welcoming place.

Joja sat down on a small wooden stool by the fire. The Wise Woman made some honey-sweet herbal tea for them both, and then she too sat by the fireside.

Joja spoke first:

'I so wanted to meet you. I am not happy in my life. I thought you might help me.' Joja was becoming tearful and her words trailed away.

'Sometimes it is easier to talk to a stranger. I will listen and help if I can'. The Woman spoke softly.

'But first I must tell you that I know much about you already.'

'How is that possible?'

Joja was now more than a little afraid.

The Wise Woman laughed and answered her lightly.

'Only because your mother came here a long while ago! She cares greatly about you, more than you realise'.

Joja was very startled by this response and opened her eyes wide in disbelief. "Tell me what causes so much distress in one as young as you."

And so it was that Joja poured out to the Wise Woman of the Hills the tales of her childhood; her lack of any friends; her temper and discontent and all the feelings of resentment that she had in her heart.

The Wise Woman leaned forward and listened carefully.

"Oh, Joja, you are so young and want so much from life. But to be content you need to find happiness within yourself. I am sure there are many who care deeply for you, but you constantly push them away."

Joja's voice rose in self-defence.

"No-one talks of my father, my real father. And my step-father does not care about me. And some of the people even think I am cursed or evil!"

"But do you feel 'evil', my child? I can see only the hurt and pain that you give yourself. My eyes are failing but I can see into your heart and know that you have much good in you. Your mother suffered a great loss when your father was taken. It is sorrow that stops her from talking about him. I, too, have suffered such a great loss and it is difficult to speak of such things."

Joja was shaken by this. She had never imagined that her father could be dead. She had rather thought him to be an itinerant pedlar, perhaps. Or someone that no-one could speak of with any respect.

Joja changed tack.

"I have something else to tell you. Yesterday I saw a dragon. My mother does not believe me, but it is true! I saw the dragon across the sea, through the fog, and I know that it is coming here!"

The Wise Woman was clearly alarmed by this.

"The mist can play tricks on the mind. But sometimes the gods do take strange forms to warn us and maybe this was the dragon you saw."

She reached up to a shelf and took down a stone. Joja thought at first it was a bird's egg, but it was solid and strangely patterned.

"Hold this in your hand and tell me what you feel."

Joja took the egg in her hand and wrapped her fingers lightly around it. Deep warmth went through her whole body. It was as

63

though the pain and destructive thoughts that she had harboured for so long were being released from her forever. Had a curse been lifted from her? She did not believe in such things. But in herself she felt a calmness she had never known before. The Wise Woman watched closely and seemed assured by Joja's response.

"Come," said the Wise Woman, "I need to talk to your mother."

Joja stood by as the two women talked. At length it was agreed that Joja should spend time with the Wise Woman until the signs that Joja had revealed to her could be interpreted. Joja's mother hugged her tightly and Joja promised to visit her as often as the weather would allow. She walked with her mother back down to the woodland path and gave her one last hug. Then Joja returned alone to live with her new 'friend'.

But that mild autumn ended with the wildest winter in years. Bitter winds and driving rain launched themselves down from the hills onto the poor settlement below. The rain sometimes turned to hailstone, although the salty air meant snow did not lie on the ground. It was this chill and this dampness that had taken many lives in the past and the people were fearful. The night frosts were bitter and great icicles formed from the treetops and seemed never to melt completely away.

Soon it would be Samhain, the ending of the Celtic year. It would be a time of feasting; a time of settling problems and of throwing out old ideas and influences. It was a special time: October the thirty-first, the time when the veil between this world and the next would be at its thinnest.

It was the time for remembrance of their ancestors, but also a time of Divination when glimpses of the future might be found.

And it seemed that this year, Joja's dragon was to be part of that.

Chapter 22

But that winter Joja was not alone in seeing signs! Whirlwinds and sheets of lightning also brought fear to far-off communities. Driving rain meant food stocks were spoilt and there was little chance for new crops to be nurtured. No-one else saw dragons it is true, but comets with fiery tails were seen in the dark skies far out over the sea.

Famine loomed, remaining cattle were killed as they could not be fed, and all felt pressured to look out only for themselves.

Some men were meeting on a beach together. They were planning a raid on a tribe to the south. Haggad, a tall man spoke first. Like the others he was painfully thin and sick with worry about his family.

'We need food; we cannot continue like this.'

'We are warriors; we can do great deeds for our people.' The others nodded and cheers greeted his words.

'We need new land, fertile land; we need treasure to trade.'

'We have our ships and we fear no-one.'

The words spoken were fervent; all were in agreement and waved their broad swords and axes in salute to each other as they made ready for the evening tide.

Earlier exploratory sailings had given these men a daring plan, a plan that presented little risk and offered great rewards.

They returned to their families and awaited the signal. Olaf's longship would be the first to set sail. Three ships were waiting down in the harbour. Olaf had no fear as he sat with his family. Like the others he believed that the time of death was set from birth and nothing changed it. To die in battle was likely if his time was come; otherwise he would fight just as bravely and return safely to his family with the necessary plunder.

His wife was not as convinced. She knew how treacherous the seas could be.

"Please, at least, consult the Guardian first, Olaf. He will read the runes for you and decide if the time is right time for sailing".

Olaf smiled at her fears but nevertheless set off to the far side of their village to seek advice from the Guardian. He found the white haired old man sitting cross-legged outside his home. The old man looked up as he heard Olaf's boots crunching along the frosted earth. Olaf nodded to him and sat down opposite to him.

"I know why you are here," announced the ancient figure, "just give me time to prepare."

Olaf sat in silence. The Guardian carefully spread out a white cloth on the ground between them. Then he reached for the small sack of tablets. He placed them in the centre of the cloth. Then he placed his hands on the white covering and lowered his head in meditation. Olaf, knowing the ritual, did the same; he tried to visualize a successful outcome for the planned raid. He waited till the old man was ready.

The rune tablets were taken from the sack and placed face down on the cloth. The

Guardian moved them round in a circle several times before he stopped. "Take," he said and held up three fingers.

With much concentration, Olaf chose the first rune and turned it face up. The shape on it resembled a zigzag of lightning.

"Sigel, sun to the seafarer," said the Seer, stroking his beard. "It is a good omen."

Olaf gazed at the array of tablets and chose a second. This one bore the shape of an arrow, pointing upwards.

"Tir, the warrior, is ever-moving and in the darkness of night never rests." Again it seemed to be a good omen as the ancient one smiled.

The last one: Olaf hesitated. He reached out, but then drew back his hand. As he focused more intently, he now found his hand was drawn to one last tablet.

He turned it over and looked at it. He knew this one: it was Ing, so named after the first of the eastern Danes, a great sea-farer. The lozenge shaped rune suggested completion of the given task.

The old man took the three chosen runes in his hands and held them tightly. He closed his eyes and intoned a plea to the gods for clarity in his interpretation.

He then spoke to Olaf.

"The signs are in your favour. Your undertaking will be successful. The tides and the moon will be with you."

Olaf thanked him and placed a silver coin on the cloth, as he rose to leave.

He went home and embraced his wife and told her of the runes he had chosen. He kissed his two sons before making his way down towards the ships. He sounded a loud note on the large horn kept at the prow of his ship and the others came forward to his signal.

The oarsmen were already on board. They would make good time; the sea was lulled that night and the moon peeped only intermittently from between dark clouds, so bestowing merely an occasional lighted path on the waters ahead of them. Olaf the

Navigator guided them, keeping close to their home-shore for as long as possible.

Soon they had passed the most treacherous rocks. It was now time to use only the sails. They tacked silently across to the eastern shore of Northern England. They could now see the shadowy buildings and the high structure which was their goal.

They would soon be ashore.

Chapter 23

The Wise Woman was unafraid of cold and hunger, but that winter had also bought bad dreams, and auguries of impending disaster. She was restless, unable to interpret fully what was coming, but she knew it would be grim.

The Wise Woman and Joja were by the brook. Joja was leaning down to fill a jug with water when a sudden whirlwind almost swept her off her feet. The scarlet berries were ripped from the rowan tree and some of its branches fell scattered onto the cold earth. Joja and the Wise Woman hastened back to the cave as great sheets of lightning flashed across the skies above. The storm raged for several days and the Wise Woman's face grew grave. She told Joja of her dream, the dream that frightened her and came back nightly to haunt her.

"When you told me of your dragon, Joja, I knew it was a sign. Now I dream nightly of three fiery dragons that fly over our people peacefully sleeping in their homes. These dragons are breathing out long hot flames and thick smoke that blackens the sky. And each dragon seeks to bring destruction. One sets the fields ablaze; the second sets homes on fire; and the third burns the boats so all are destroyed. Nothing remains for our people. And a great wail comes up from them and no-one is there to help."

The Wise Woman was in tears as she related these terrifying omens to poor Joja. "What can we do?" asked Joja. "There must be a way to warn our people."

"This time," said the Wise Woman, "I do not have the answer. I fear greatly what is to come."

In this time of great fear, Joja found herself seeking solace in the words her mother had taught her about the love and compassion of the Son of God. The Wise Woman had the power to predict calamities and desolation; but she offered neither comfort nor resources to cope with whatever lay ahead. Joja felt strongly the need for her mother.

'Why don't we both return to our people and help them', she begged.

The Wise Woman looked distraught. She felt panic yet knew she should go and offer her aid to those that lived below in the settlement.

At length she replied, 'If the weather eases and my nightmares still seek fulfilment, then I will go back with you and see what can be done.'

Joja tried to sleep but her thoughts were with her mother, her kind, caring and loving mother.

She just wanted to go back home.

Chapter 24

Brother Bartram looked down at his fingers. They were swollen and stiff. He cupped them together and blew into them hoping his breath would bring some life back to them.

He had prepared the large initial letter for the page and the imagery of leaves and flowers around it was ready for colour to be added. He could do no more that day. He visualized the gold leaf, red berry ink and seaweed green that he would use to complete his work and was pleased. He covered his wooden pots of ink and his work and mumbled a prayer to call a blessing on his labours. He extinguished the candle near his workplace and he made his way to the long dining room.

Other monks were leaving their work and he joined them by the bowl and pitcher of water laid ready by the youngest monk. He dipped his fingers in only briefly; the water was icy cold! He dried them on the proffered cloth and went to sit down in his usual place. And soon the dining room was filled with monks all seated expectantly around the rough-hewn wooden table.

The smell of warm bread and soup was welcoming and the monks were ready to relax. After 'grace', they were able to talk to one another; this was not a silent order and it was the time of day they most enjoyed.

'Well, Brother Absalom, your bread is too hard today! You want me to break my teeth?' teased the oldest monk among them.

They all laughed at this for Brother Absalom was renowned, even on the mainland, for his great bread-making! He had just the right touch and better still, he never wasted any of the precious flour and there was always bread enough even if sometimes there was little to go with it.

Some of the monks who looked after the monastery gardens expressed their fears that the water-logged earth meant remaining root crops were rotting; and there was little chance that early sowings could take place that year. It had been a dreadful winter. But these monks were not in want. They were the lucky recipients of numerous donations from wealthy patrons! Not only sacks of grain, the best fruits of the harvest, the best fish caught and other such gifts from nearby communities, but they also had treasure! Kings, and 'would-be' kings had endowed their chapel with silver candlesticks, white altar cloths of purest silk embroidered in gold, golden platters and a huge gold cross studded with blood-red rubies. There were also exquisitely carved wooden screens and a pulpit of solid oak. The gifts were good, but the motives of the donors were dubious! Whilst not seeking to 'buy a place in heaven', a gift was often made to placate the Christian God and ask for help in securing their vaulted ambitions! Why not? It had worked in the old days, when sacrifices were made to the gods before battle!

Their simple meal over, the monks made their way to the chapel for evening prayers. The night was dark but the sea, which had raged for several days without cease, seemed strangely quiet that night.

They were all facing the altar, shaven heads bowed, when they heard the first crashing sounds. The huge arched door behind them broke open, shattered by heavy axe-blows!

Haggad now stood framed where the door had been. At least ten other axemen were behind him. These men looked like giants in their tall helmets and thick tunics. Fierce angry words spoken in a strange language made them even more terrifying; but alas, their intent was all too easily understood.

The shock was unimaginable! Heathen pirates stormed into the small chapel and the good monks had no means of escape. They yelled out transfixed in shock and terror, momentarily unable to make any attempt to defend themselves or to get away.

The wooden bench where Brother Bartram had been seated was suddenly felled with a mighty blow. It split in two throwing all the monks down onto the floor. As the monk right next to him fell, Bartram saw blood flowing from a sword wound to his neck. It was Olaf's sword which had quickly been dispatched to demolish the poor innocent man. Some monks managed to crawl into hiding in the crypt, but others were slain right there in the holy sanctuary. One monk bravely stepped forward and spread out his arms to try to save the holy cross of rubies and gold. He, too, was brought down by a heavy sword and fell even onto the altar, staining the white cloth with his life's blood.

A horn sounded and the raiders were distracted for an instant. Bartram ran to the side door which led to the outer cloisters and his workplace. He pulled up his hood and tried to hide in the shadowy archways. By this means, he managed to reach the oaken box that was the repository for completed manuscripts. He could not see, but by touch he knew they were all safe and as he had left them. He made his way to his table and put his hand under the covering cloth. Yes, his work was still undamaged. He hid behind his oak desk, praying fervently that he would not be discovered.

Three blasts now came from a horn somewhere out there in the darkness. As swift as the attack was, the withdrawal was even faster. Had it really happened? The raiders came and went in a seeming instant! But they had paused just long enough to throw down their flaming torches. They were leaving behind death and destruction as had never been seen before: a scene that surely seemed to come from Hell itself.

As the loud screams of terror echoed that night, brave men from the mainland attempted to cross to the Priory. The tide was out, so the causeway was flooded. Small boats were launched in great haste but the rowers were shocked back as flames from Lindisfarne reached high into the heavens. Two young monks were rescued from the swirling water and quicksand but little more could be done.

The smoke and flames now reached Brother Bartram's hiding place. He tried desperately to douse the leaping flames that would soon engulf the precious parchments, but it was futile. His hands were burned in the effort and the smoke billowing out in great clouds, blinded and choked him. Brother Bartram's dying thoughts were of the letter remaining; the one he would have delighted in gilding the following day; a day that now had been taking from him forever.

Chapter 25

Other 'would-be raiders' were also meeting on the beach, but this time at Craghburn. Desperate times called for desperate measures.

"We should raid neighbouring settlements. Our people are starving." This was Joja's eldest step-brother.

Bren, no longer round-faced and jovial, had children and grandchildren to provide for. But he did not like the plans being put forward.

"No-one has enough food," he sighed. "But what right have we to steal from others?"

Bren shook his head sadly. Others were quick to sneer.

"Have you a better idea, then? Or shall we just watch our children starve?"

"My family have only dried fish and seaweed left. And we have little flour to make bread."

An old man spoke wearily.

"The brook is still frozen; only the underground spring-water saves us. My daughter lies sick with fever and hunger."

"Maybe there will be a break in the weather, soon," Bren countered. "Will our remaining cattle survive that long? They are starving too."

Joja's step-brother was unconvinced.

Bren spoke the only words he could offer:

"Spring must surely come!" It was a forlorn hope.

The discussion and recriminations went on late that night. The group of men wandered aimlessly along the sands.

But then their attention became riveted elsewhere!

A great blaze had appeared in the heavens and its bright-red glow could be seen to the right of the bay but far off. In the darkness they were afraid. They knew not what had happened but their eyes were drawn towards 'the islands of the strong winds': the Farne islands. And the largest island there was a holy sanctuary, the priory of Lindisfarne!

Despite their fears they scrambled up onto the rocks and gazed out across the dark sea. Strange loud noises carried on the wind and they smelt the smoke now billowing out from that red glow. Was it indeed the end of the world that Streng had said would surely come in their lifetime? Only monks lived there on Lindisfarne, monks who spent their time in contemplation, who worked diligently to compile beautiful records of the Scriptures, and lived lives that were exemplary in every aspect. What disruption could possible afflict such a place! Was the Judgement Day to begin there?

All plans to raid another tribe were abandoned. The men ran back to their homes and sought safety for their families. They had no way of knowing what had taken place that night, and it was to be several days before a messenger arrived in Craghburn with the dreadful news.

Chapter 26

It was Streng's young son who came on horseback to the frightened people. At the sound of galloping hooves the men gathered together in the open place behind the houses. They could see from his pale face and sorrowful eyes that he did indeed have dreadful tidings to relate.

"They came to the Priory," he burst out. "The monks are slain; the altars ripped out and sacred emblems taken from them by force!"

Who could have done these terrible deeds? The men found it hard to take in what he tried to tell them.

"Who did this abomination?"

"Who could so defile the holy places?" "Where is your father? Is he safe?"

Women and children came out to the sounds of distress and some fell to their knees at what they heard.

Streng's son got down from his horse; some-one gave him water to drink and he began again.

"They came from the north at night. No-one heard them come. Their ships came stealthily right up to the shore and then they sounded horns and shouted in rage as they attacked the monks at prayer."

The people were shocked into silence.

"They killed the monks?" one man asked in horror.

"Many monks are dead. Some managed to flee, but others tried to protect the holy treasures and were slain even at the altar. And when they had taken all, even the gold cross, then they threw down their flaming torches and set the whole priory alight!"

The community could not believe that this could have happened. Why would God have let this happen to the good monks? What had they done? Was this a punishment? And who would be next?

"But what of your father? Where is Streng?"

"He went back with some of the monks who fled. They have taken Cuthbert's remains to a safe place and he is with them."

Streng's young son remained with them for only one night. He set off again to take his devastating message to other settlements.

Behind him he left a community stunned and terrified; a community that dared not scan the horizon for fear that the same fate would be manifest on the very shores of Craghburn!

Chapter 27

There was terror throughout the area, throughout the country; terror that was to spread even further as news of the events of that fateful night was relayed throughout the Christian world. When would the heathen pirates return? Who would be next? If evil could come to such a holy place then all must fear God's wrath. Or had these raiders been sent by Satan himself?

The people of Craghburn met in fear. They did not have Streng to guide them. They huddled below the sand dunes and tried to decide what to do. Some wanted to abandon their settlement and take their chances in the hills.

"We cannot remain here near the shore. We will be an easy target!"

But most were reluctant to leave and many were too weak to make the journey. Others remembered Streng's words to them.

"We have failed to listen," they reasoned.

"We cling to the old ways and we will be punished."

The Spring festival was approaching: a time of cleansing and renewal. Perhaps this was the answer. Maybe they still had time to change their ancient rites and follow the new Christian religion more closely. Could their faith be strengthened and would God have mercy and save them? Or was Judgement Day indeed coming and bringing with it the greater need for cleansing of their souls!

As they talked, Joja and the Wise Woman were making their way across the fields.

Joja was leading the Wise Woman who was walking slowly with the aid of a stick.

Neither was aware of the events that had taken place at Lindisfarne; nor of the welcome they were about to receive.

They came close to the dunes and started to make their descent. A woman jumped up as she saw their approach.

"The Wise Woman is evil. She keeps the old ways. She sees signs but is it by magic or by demons? Where do her gifts come from?"

Others, too, began to mutter against her. The raid on the holy island had shaken everyone. They now saw evil all around them and each one strove to gain only personal salvation.

The Wise Woman stood in silence. She was shaken that she could be the focus of their distrust and fears. Many were equally horrified but were afraid to speak out. They remembered her kindness to them in days of trouble and had seen no harm in her. The Wise Woman looked sorely distressed. Was it the accusations now being made? Or was she re-living a greater grief as she gazed at that once-familiar shore?

Just then the Wise Woman looked up to the slowly darkening sky. It was almost nightfall and a strange light seemed to drop from the heavens. It was a falling star! The worst of omens! A portent that filled all the onlookers there with the greatest of dread: the sign of impending death! It surely heralded the end of their world.

The people as one fell to the ground: some in prayer; some still grasping the special 'lucky' stones they had kept from the old days. It was too late now to choose.

Only the Wise Woman and Joja were still standing. Joja saw the Wise Woman walk towards the rocks in a trance as though transfixed by something she had seen beyond the sky above. Joja hesitated, and then tried to follow her. But she was too far behind her. She could only watch as the Wise Woman clambered upwards, without her stick and looking only above her. Joja saw her reached the topmost rock, raise her hands to the heavens, and heard her calling out one name only: Dani.

But then there came a heart-rending scream as the Wise Woman lost her footing. She slipped and fell from the highest rock into the deep ocean below.

Others too heard her scream and swore that the Wise Woman had spoken a curse that would remain on Craghburn forever.

PART THREE

Chapter 28

"See you later, then, Kate. Have a good time!"

Katy grimaced. She held out her hand and looked at the sky. It was already drizzling. Not the best of days to explore the Roman Wall!

Georgia waved her off, and began to prepare for her own 'expedition'. Unlike Katy, Georgia was not a History student, but nevertheless she'd decided to join the student excursion to Northumberland along with the others, but for very different reasons. Armed with an old postcard, some black and white family photos, and a wealth of anecdotes and memories from her grandparents, she was off to find the small bay of Craghburn, a place she had heard so much about but had never before visited.

And so her odyssey now began. The bus no longer meandered through small towns and villages offering glimpses of Northumbrian open spaces and greenery, as she had been told. Disappointingly, this route was now by dual carriageway, a road like so many others; it could have been anywhere. It was a speedy route but a dreary experience in the now quite heavy rain.

She sat close to the window as the bus now branched off uphill. At last the surrounding countryside stretched out before her and the high dark hills loomed behind as they always had. The bus was now heading towards the coast, but a mist-hidden coastline it was to be.

She pictured her Grandfather in his old Austin and the primus stove that Grandma said he'd taken everywhere! And she remembered the tales she'd heard of picnics in the hillsides; a drive across to Holy

Island in a snowstorm one Easter when the children had wondered if they'd be marooned there for the rest of the holiday!

Her Grandmother's family came mainly from the Border country: some were very definitely Scottish, and some Northumbrian. Grandma had been born in Craghburn which in her day was a fishing village. She'd told young Georgia many a tale of the fisher folk and their superstitions. There was never to be whistling on board any boat or ship: you might whistle up a ferocious wind! No self-respecting fishermen ever set sail on the thirteenth of the month and especially not Friday the thirteenth! Women on board were also considered 'unlucky' and the word 'pig' was never to be used, though no-one knew why! Should this word be used by accident in conversation, any fisherman who overheard it would turn back home rather than risk going to sea that day.

After church or chapel her grandmother's family, and most of the other families, would walk along the then newly built promenade in their Sunday finery. And the Summer time brought fairgrounds and Punch and Judy stalls and once "even a Pierrot show, live on the sands." Georgia had never been quite sure what a Pierrot show was, but it seemed to be a favourite memory of her Grandmother's, so it would have been rude to ask!

The church up near the moors housed a very old graveyard and Grandma said that an ancient tomb stone there, shaped as a large stone table, had a dreadful tradition attached to it. It was said that if you placed a pin on the table and ran around it three times, then the devil himself would appear!

"Did anyone do that?" Georgia had asked wide-eyed.

"No-one was that brave!" her Grandmother had replied. "One boy just put a pin on the table and we all ran away terrified".

Somewhere further back in her Grandfather's family there was an Irish connection, and he had inherited 'the Blarney' side at least! His 'stories' were word-pictures that meandered in so many directions before 'getting to the point'. Georgia smiled to herself as she thought of him. She'd always been her Granddad's favourite!

His weirdest story though, was of a great-aunt who lived 'up in the hills'. No-one ever saw her, unless some great disaster was impending! She would then descend with her 'retinue of maids' as he called it, and arrive on the relevant doorstep declaring: you are going to need me!

Georgia's Grandfather was impressed that this relative's 'sixth sense' was infallible: death or disaster duly arrived! Georgia privately thought this relative couldn't expect much of a welcome! Anyone with any sense would have shut the door in her face!

Craghburn began to appear on road signs, but she saw little to recognise. Housing estates were spread for miles, and whatever coastline there was had been blocked from view by continuous building programmes. Most passengers left the bus at the next stop, a bustling town with modern shops and a large bus station. This could not be Craghburn, could it?

The driver stopped her: your stop is further on. We're not there yet.

The road now narrowed; there was little other traffic; and she was alone with the driver. No bus station it seemed, but this was it: one stop on the main street.

A few dingy shops clung like limpets to the edge of the long crescent of large terraced houses; houses that had been much-sought after in their day as they fronted onto the promenade; houses that her Grandmother's had generation aspired to. A large central shop was painted bright yellow but the cheap paint was already peeling off. It seemed to be a newsagent's and sandwich bar and video shop all rolled into one! Next to it was a Chinese Takeaway; then a Tattooist that also offered body-piercing! One shop was closed down completely with boarded-up windows that were covered in graffiti; another clothes shop proclaimed massive reductions in its 'closing down' sale. Drab jumpers and limp skirts stood on rails outside but there seemed to be few takers. Jake's fruit and vegetables were on display further down. Jake appeared unable to spell 'lettuce' and his handwritten prices suggested he sold 'collies' too.

In between all this was a rusty sign: to the Beach.

Chapter 29

Although the rain had now stopped and there was no wind, the beach was completely deserted. Stone steps beside the sand-dunes were still there, but the sand-dunes themselves were not as she had imagined. The sand seemed grimy and dingy; not the white sand of her grandparents' fond memories, and it was even worse at the lower edges. Litter was festooned the length of the once famed dunes: plastic bags; torn off coloured wrappers; cardboard containers of every shape and size and the plastic cutlery that must have come with them; broken swimming goggles; beach towels and tissues; spades without handles and burst beach balls: eggshell and even odd shoes! All had been carelessly discarded or deliberately left behind! Did no-one care? It was a messy collection and a dreadful insight into hundreds of past picnics. Worse: discarded condoms gave evidence of many illicit trysts having taken place amongst the long grasses. Georgia did not look too closely but no doubt there were discarded needles down there too! It was revolting! No child would be allowed to slide down those dunes; no child would even want to!

She hurried past, down to the beach and walked close to the water's edge. Dull yellowish foam spat up from a muddy sea. A dead seagull lay at her feet. It was grotesque; like some sort of nightmare. She climbed on to the flat rocks and gazed down into the rock pools. There was nothing moving in any of them, not even a hermit crab. They were just pools of dark brown still water with nothing alive in them! And from the rocks she saw below, where the sea rushed between the rock spaces forming small gullies: dead fish! There were about a dozen of them, floating upwards on the surface and being buffeted by each wave that came.

She looked across towards the old church that still stood to the north. The moors visible behind it seemed to serve as a scrap yard, a burial ground for broken down cars. The church still looked impressive even at this distance. It was exactly like the postcard that she now took from her pocket. "Rebuilt in Victorian times, this church was built on the site of a much more ancient church", she read.

A figure had appeared from amongst the lower rocks; a figure that seemed to be clothed all in white! After a while another figure joined the first one. And this one too was clothed in white! They were close together now and looking down at a box that the first one was carrying. They did not look like ghosts. They were more like aliens! Very strange!

Georgia gazed back at the sand dunes and felt tears sting her eyes. It was as though a curse had befallen this place once so sacred to her family's history.

She climbed back to the top and sat on a bench. Most of the good people of Craghburn were piling into their cars and setting off to find somewhere better to spend their weekend!

Chapter 30

An old man with a small white dog ambled to the front of the promenade rails. He sighed as he looked down over the bay.

Georgia waited, thinking perhaps she should visit the church and be able to relate that, at least, to her Grandma.

"Is the church open to visitors?" she asked him.

"Nay, hinnie. It's been boarded up for three years or more. Look there, see them rocks, yonder? They used to go out another mile beyond the church. The sea's reclaiming aal of it. Them rocks is aal but covered. The church'll be next to gan!"

"Was it once a lovely bay? My family came from here and they always said so."

"It was perfect. The sands were clean; the pools full of crabs and starfish. And there were fishing boats aal alang there." He pointed towards the moor.

"What has happened?"

"Whey man, the coal mining and the power station, fer starters! But look, see those men in white? They're testing for radiation on the beach. Drifted down from Scotland, aa bet! Nuclear submarines, most like. It's an aa'ful shame! We had good times here when aa was young!"

Georgia stared out to the sea, and tried to visualize how it must have been. The old man shuffled off.

"Take care then, hinnie."

"You too!" she called after him.

Her mobile rang and she checked the text.

"Rain stopped. Roman Wall brill! C u soon. Katy X"

At least, someone was having a good day!

There was no sign of a bus. She checked at the bus stop: an hour to wait. Georgia was filled with an overwhelming urge to leave the place as soon as ever could be possible. The newsagent now had a sign posted outside: Tests for radioactivity on local beach positive! She went in a bought the local paper and a bottle of water.

She sat at the bus stop to read it.

It was indeed Craghburn they meant. A couple had been interviewed and maintained that their dog had died as a result of their regular walks on the beach. Other 'locals' commented on the dearth of any living creature in the rock pools: fishermen spoke of shoals of dead fish further off the coast.

Craghburn was surely cursed.

Chapter 31

The hostel was still deserted when Georgia returned. The History students were still out on their field trip.

She made herself a cup of coffee in the tiny communal kitchen and went to sit down on the bed. She laid out the photographs and the postcard of the church at Craghburn on the quilt cover. Should she take the local paper back for her grandparents? They would be so shocked when she told them of her impression of Craghburn!

Katy's bed was still unmade; she'd rushed out that morning, late as usual! Georgia went across to straighten the covers and to move Katy's clothes on to the chair near the window.

On the desk in the corner, Katy's files and books were scattered. Katy was a brilliant student; a real 'high flyer' but Georgia often wondered how she ever completed any work: she was so disorganised!

"Better not to move any of it, though," she thought. All the small scraps of paper with hand-written notes were probably vital to Katy's final thesis. Only Katy knew how they all fitted together.

Georgia was an Art student and noted for her meticulous work. She could not function in Katy's ways! A small paperback book, half-hidden under Katy's file caught her attention.

The cover of the book was a coloured depiction of Celtic Art. A circle predominated, but strong bands of colour were carefully interwoven around this. Even Georgia's trained 'eye', found it difficult to follow these strands as they looped in and out of each other in an intricate pattern. She read the wording to the cover plate: Celtic knot design. The circle and unbroken strands represent the old symbols for eternity.

The book title was *'Celtic Myths and Legends'*

Georgia took the book to her bedside chair and picked up her coffee. She began by reading the foreword page. Before giving accounts of the Celtic gods and heroes, and all their adventures, the book gave this warning:-

'Balb, an ancient Irish goddess was said to have foretold the coming end of the Age of the gods. Her prophecy foretold the end of the divine age and the beginning of a new one:

An age when summers would be flowerless and cows give no milk; When women would be shameless and men be without strength;

In which there would be trees without fruit and seas without fish;

When old men would give false judgement and legislators would make unjust laws; When warriors would betray one another and men would be thieves and there would be no more virtue left in the world!'

Georgia read it over again. She'd already seen the 'seas without fish.' Had Balb truly predicted the demise of the Age of the gods?

Or was she addressing another more godless age entirely?

The circle was almost complete.

ABOUT THE AUTHOR

Born in Northumberland, eldest of four children. Began 'teaching' in backyard at a very early age! Married with three grown-up children – a boy and two girls. Two grand-daughters.

Ex-primary schoolteacher; have also taught English to foreign students. Began writing at age of eight (or so mother reckons!), contributed to college magazine and 'dabbled' with plays and poetry.

Mostly writing factual accounts. Learned how 'do research' during fight to save local playing field from developers. As a result was given regular monthly column on local current affairs on-line magazine. Worked as a free-lance proofreader whilst continuing with my own writing.